MEET THE MAYOR/
CONOCE A LOS ALCALDES

By Joyce Jeffries   Traducción al español: Eduardo Alamán

Gareth Stevens
Publishing

Please visit our website, www.garethstevens.com. For a free color catalog of all our high-quality books, call toll free 1-800-542-2595 or fax 1-877-542-2596.

Library of Congress Cataloging-in-Publication Data

Jeffries, Joyce.
Meet the mayor = Conoce a los alcaldes / by Joyce Jeffries.
  p. cm. — (People around town = Gente de mi ciudad)
Parallel title: Conoce a los alcaldes
In English and Spanish.
Includes index.
ISBN 978-1-4339-9470-8 (library binding)
1. Mayors—Juvenile literature. 2. Occupations—Juvenile literature. I. Jeffries, Joyce. II. Title.
JS141.N34 2013
352.23'216–dc23

First Edition

Published in 2014 by
Gareth Stevens Publishing
111 East 14th Street, Suite 349
New York, NY 10003

Editor: Ryan Nagelhout
Designer: Nicholas Domiano

Photo credits: Cover, pp. 1, 5 Photos.com/Thinkstock.com; p. 5 Iakov Filimonov/Shutterstock.com; pp. 7, 19 iStockphoto/Thinkstock.com; pp. 9, 24 Hemera/Thinkstock.com; p. 11 Creatas/Thinkstock.com; p 13 Janne Hamalainen/Shutterstock.com; p. 15 ben bryant/Shutterstock.com; p. 17 Andersen Ross/Blend Images/Getty Images; p. 19 Huntstock/Thinkstock.com; pp. 21 , 23 & 24 (speech) Digital Vision/Thinkstock.com; p. 24 (money) Africa Studio/Shutterstock.com.

Printed in the United States of America

CPSIA compliance information: Batch #CS13GS: For further information contact Gareth Stevens, New York, New York at 1-800-542-2595.

Contents

Contenido

Mayors run towns!

¡Los alcaldes son los jefes de las ciudades y los pueblos!

They are part
of the government.

Forman parte del
gobierno.

They work at city hall.

Trabajan en la alcaldía.

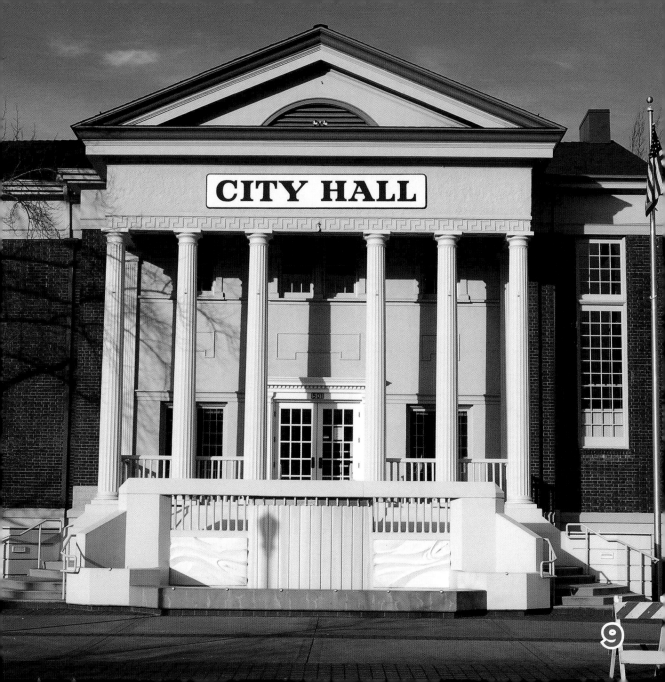

People vote them into office.

Son elegidos por la gente.

REGISTER HERE

11

They help fix problems
in town.

Los alcaldes resuelven
los problemas de las
ciudades.

They help make rules.
These are called laws.

Ayudan a crear las
reglas. Estas reglas son
las leyes.

20
M.P.H.
W13-1   DEPT OF TRANSPORTATION

STOP

NO
PARKING
ANY TIME

15

Laws keep us safe!

¡Las leyes nos
mantienen seguros!

They pick how a town
uses its money.

Los alcaldes deciden
cómo se usa el dinero
en la ciudad.

19

They speak for the city.

Hablan en nombre
de la ciudad.

20

They talk to people
about the city.
This is called a speech.

Hablan sobre la
ciudad. A esto se le
llama discurso.

Words to Know/
Palabras que debes saber

city hall/
(la) alcaldía

money/
(el) dinero

speech/
(el) discurso

Index / Índice